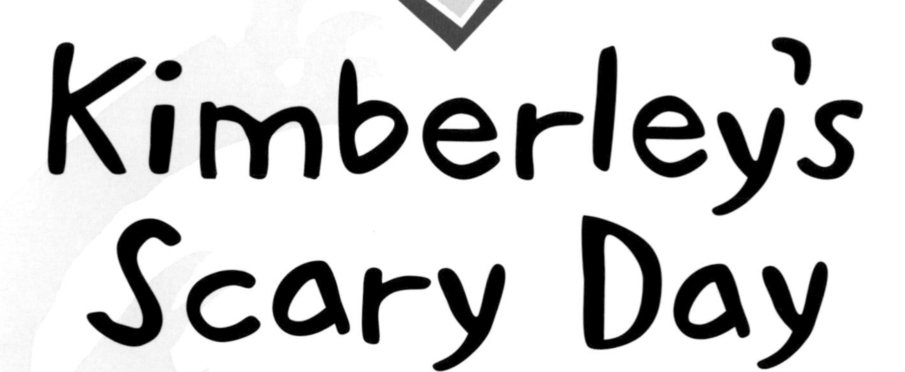

Kimberley's Scary Day

Written by
Ann Bryant

Illustrated by
Ross Collins

W
FRANKLIN WATTS
LONDON • SYDNEY

Ann Bryant

"I love walking, especially in forests. I haven't come across Foxy yet, thank goodness!"

Ross Collins

"I enjoy watching movies and walking our dog, Willow, at Loch Lomond. I like guinea pigs, but I couldn't eat a whole one."

Kimberley Guinea Pig went out one day
For a walk in the neighbourhood.

Sadly young Kimberley
quite lost her way ...

... And found herself deep in the Wild Wood.

Now guinea pigs aren't really known for their brains.

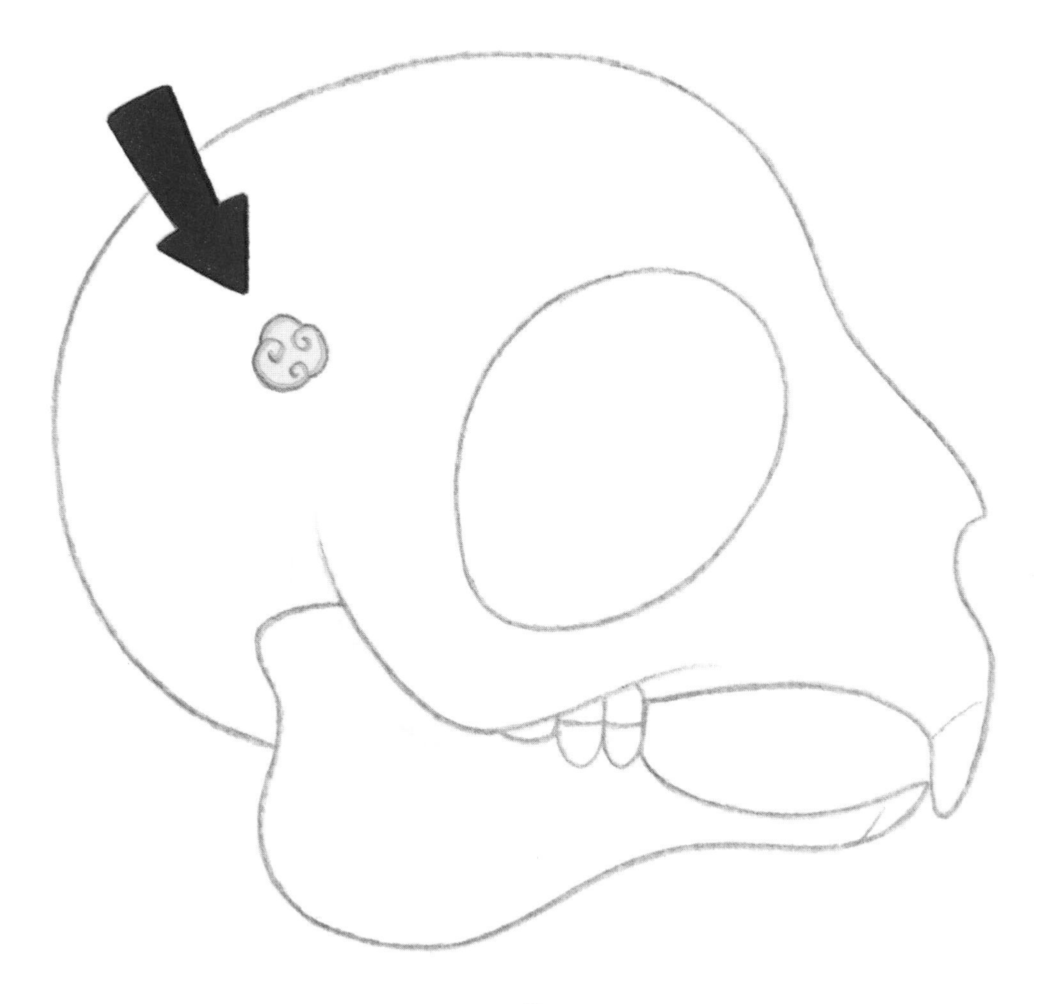

They don't make detectives ...

... or spies.

So when a smart gentleman
walked up to her,

Young Kimberley missed

the disguise.

"How do you do?"
Foxy licked his thin lips,
And showed all his teeth
as he smiled.

"My name is Kenneth.
I'm well known round here."

"I'm Kim ...

... I'm not used to the wild."

“This is my house.”

Foxy opened his door.

"Please, my dear, *do* step inside."

Kimberley smiled.

“You’re too kind, sir, I’m sure!”

Foxy imagined her fried.

Then Foxy was gone
and the kettle was on,
When Kimberley stared up
in fright.

"Oh goodness! It's him!
It's the fox with the grin
That could swallow me
all in one bite!"

Kimberley knew she
must quickly escape.
But she'd only just
got to the door ...

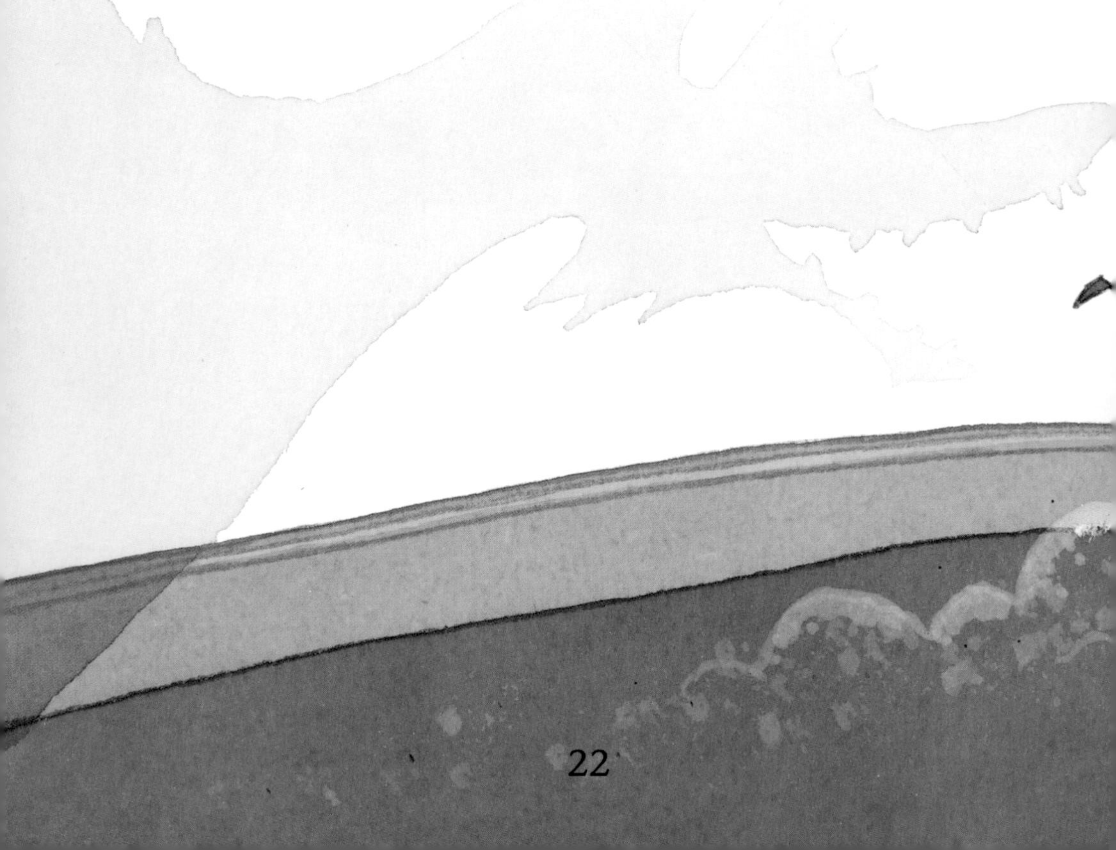

COOKING
GUINEA
PIGS
FOR ONE

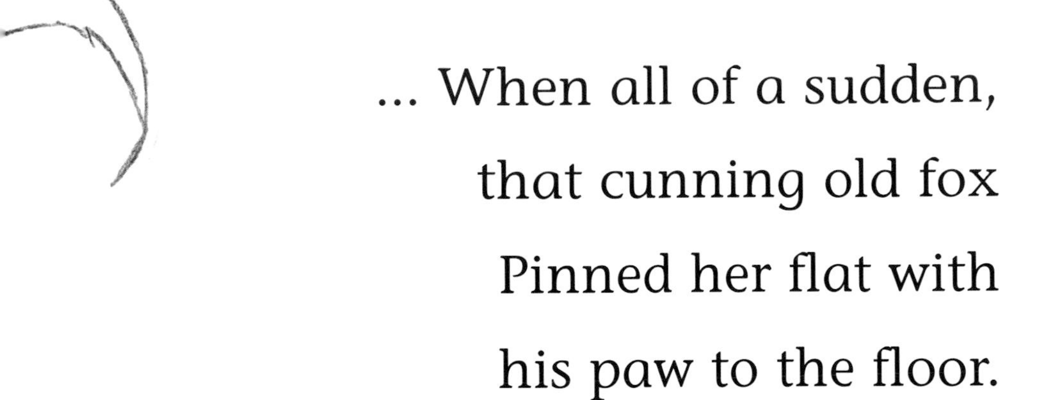

... When all of a sudden,
that cunning old fox
Pinned her flat with
his paw to the floor.

From outside the door
came a terrible growl
And the voice
of the Big Daddy Bear.

"Let go of her, Foxy.

Let go right now!

Or I'll eat you for supper,

I swear!"

“You’re safe,” said the bear.
“I’ll take you home now,
Away from this horrible fox.

There's someone outside
who'll be great as a guide ..."

"... Kimberley, meet Goldilocks!"

PORRIDGE

Notes for parents and teachers

READING CORNER has been structured to provide maximum support for new readers. The stories may be used by adults for sharing with young children. Primarily, however, the stories are designed for newly independent readers, whether they are reading these books in bed at night, or in the reading corner at school or in the library.

Starting to read alone can be a daunting prospect. READING CORNER helps by providing visual support and repeating words and phrases, while making reading enjoyable. These books will develop confidence in the new reader, and encourage a love of reading that will last a lifetime!

If you are reading this book with a child, here are a few tips:

1. Make reading fun! Choose a time to read when you and the child are relaxed and have time to share the story.

2. Encourage children to reread the story, and to retell the story in their own words, using the illustrations to remind them what has happened.

3. Give praise! Remember that small mistakes need not always be corrected.

READING CORNER covers three grades of early reading ability, with three levels at each grade. Each level has a certain number of words per story, indicated by the number of bars on the spine of the book, to allow you to choose the right book for a young reader:

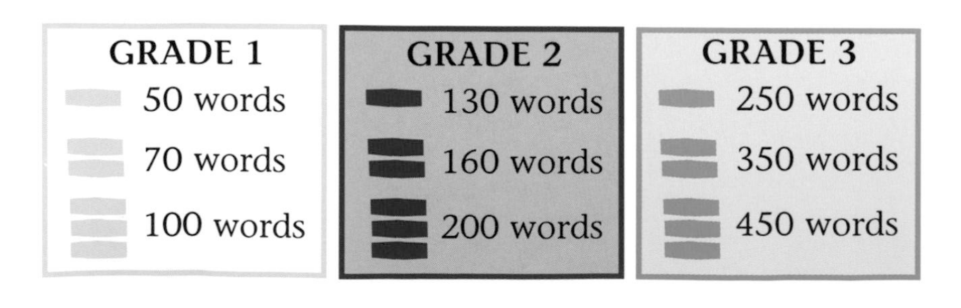